THE MYTHICS

MARINA AND THE KRAKEN

LAUREN MAGAZINER
ILLUSTRATED BY MIRELLE ORTEGA

 KATHERINE TEGEN BOOKS
An Imprint of HarperCollins Publishers

Katherine Tegen Books is an imprint of HarperCollins Publishers.

The Mythics #1: Marina and the Kraken
Text copyright © 2022 by Lauren Magaziner
Illustrations copyright © 2022 by Mirelle Ortega
information address HarperCollins Children's Books, a division of
HarperCollins Publishers, 195 Broadway, New York, NY 10007.
www.harpercollinschildrens.com

Library of Congress Control Number: 2022934211
ISBN 978-0-06-305888-0

Typography by Laura Mock
22 23 24 25 26   PC/LSCH   10 9 8 7 6 5 4 3 2 1

First Edition

TERRAFAMILIAR

LAVASIDE ROCKS

MOUNTAINSIDE SNOWS

SPLASHSIDE FALLS

SEASIDE SANDS

TUNDRASIDE FROSTS

WOODSIDE TIMBERS

PRAIRIESIDE MEADOWS

RIVERSIDE REEDS

CLIFFSIDE LEDGES

SAVANNASIDE GRASSES

SWAMPSIDE SHRUBS

DESERTSIDE DUNES

JUNGLESIDE VINES

LAKESIDE MUDS

WATERSIDE ISLES

N
W · E
S

PAIRING DAY

This is what everyone was waiting for.

"Achem!" Mayor Mejor cleared her throat. "Don't be scared, young ones," she said to the crowd of ten-year-olds. "You all look nervous. So let me make you feel better: This is only the most important day of your lives. Whatever happens today will affect your whole future. And every citizen from three towns will be watching you during the ceremony.

There, that made you feel better, didn't it?"

Marina, sitting in the back of the gym, felt like her insides were wriggling. And she wasn't the only one. Every kid in the room stared at the mayor in horror.

"In a moment, we will walk outside, and you will bond with an animal who will be with you for your whole life. This animal is called a *familiar*. Your fam—*yes, Peckadilly?*" she said to the woodpecker sitting on top of her beehive hairdo. Peckadilly had begun to hammer at her hair. Mayor Mejor looked annoyed.

"I would *die* if I got a woodpecker, wouldn't you?" a girl in front of Marina whispered to her friend. Marina could only see her from the back. She had smooth black hair that ended sharply just above her shoulders.

Her friend—a blond boy—nodded vigorously.

Marina thought they might be from Riverside Reeds or Woodside Timbers—the neighboring regions. Pairing Day happened once a year, every year, all over Terrafamiliar. Every ten-year-old in the world got their animal companion on this day.

Nearby towns usually gathered together in one spot. This year, it was Seaside Sands's turn to host Riverside Reeds and Woodside Timbers. Marina was grateful to be home. It was her best shot at getting the familiar she wanted.

Marina clasped her hands together. She was ready to beg the universe for a nice and safe familiar. All she ever wanted was a cute, harmless turtle. Or a starfish. Or an otter.

She wanted something from the ocean, like her family had. When her mom was alive, she'd had a shrimp. Her dad had a crab. Her brother, Harbor, had a sea lion.

She *needed* something from the ocean. How could she feel like part of her own family without a sea creature?

"Pairing Day is special," Mayor Mejor said, feeding Peckadilly a treat. "Can you feel it? Do you know what makes today different?"

Yes, Marina thought. Today made her want to hurl. Even more so than usual.

"Today, Terrafamiliar is closest to the sun," the mayor explained. "Not only is this the longest and brightest day of the year, it's also the day with the biggest surge in magic. The animals respond to that outpouring, and—without realizing it—you respond to it too. In a few moments, we will head outside, and the familiars will start arriving."

Marina closed her eyes and begged the universe. *Please, please*—a seahorse would be perfect. Or a seal. Or a penguin. She would even take a walrus to go with Harbor's sea lion. And (she almost couldn't dare dream it) what if she got a shrimp, just like her mom? To have that connection to her mom again . . . it would bring more comfort than she could even describe.

But terrible thoughts kept coming into Marina's head. She couldn't stop them. They all started with the words, *What if?*

What if she got a lion that was *not* from the sea? Could she handle a land lion? What if she got a scary animal? One with pointy teeth and a hunger for humans. Or even worse, what if she got a slug or worm? What if she got a cockroach?

"Your familiar resembles your personality," Mayor Mejor explained.

Oh, great. Now it would be even *worse* to get a cockroach. It gave her something else to worry about.

"So think very hard about presenting your best selves, children."

Marina twisted her hair nervously. What was her best self? She was always worried. She even worried

in her sleep. There were so many bad things that could happen. It took a lot of energy to worry about them all.

"You don't have to do anything to find your familiar. Your match will come to you, no matter what you do. All you have to do is be approachable."

Marina winced. She was sitting alone, with no one on either side of her. How in the world was she supposed to be approachable? She leaned over across an empty seat to say hi to a boy named Wade from her lower-school class.

He looked at her with mild curiosity. But his eyes felt like lasers. She was melting under the pressure. What if she talked too much? What if she talked too little? What if she said something weird or embarrassing? What if everyone secretly hated her?

"Marina? Did you want something?" Wade asked.

"Um . . . never mind," she whispered.

If she wasn't good at socializing with people, would she be any good at socializing with her familiar?

Marina curled a lock of hair around her finger and tried to focus on Mayor Mejor. She was saying something important, and Marina was too buried in her own head to hear.

"—even the venomous, dangerous, deadly animals come in peace. They mean you no harm. They're just looking for their humans."

Venomous animals? Dangerous animals? *Deadly* animals? Marina slunk down in her seat.

"Oh!" Mayor Mejor gasped, looking at her pocket watch. "The sun is almost at its highest point. It's time!" She swatted at Peckadilly, who now tried to hammer her ear. "File out, quickly now!"

Everyone rushed for the doors in the back of the gym. Marina was swept up in a current of kids, who led her into the hallway.

This is where Harbor went to school. She would go here too, once she had her familiar.

The upper school seemed made for any type of familiar. If she had a giraffe or elephant, their heads wouldn't even come close to brushing the forty-foot-tall ceilings. If she had a reptile, she could let it soak up lamplight in one of the terrarium stands. If she had a gerbil, hamster, or mouse, she would let it run wild in the walls made of multicolored plastic tubes.

Marina was too busy looking at the intertwining tubes, and she nearly tripped over a bale of hay on

the floor for the farm animals.

"Watch it!" a kid behind her said.

Marina turned around. "Sorry—"

Splash!

She stepped into an inflatable puddle pool. The kids around her laughed, and Marina blushed. Her right shoe was soaked. But at least she knew where her water familiar would paddle around.

Please let me have a water familiar, Marina thought. She passed by classrooms, and she peeked in as she was whisked by. Each room looked like it had been stretched in every direction. Her stomach knotted. What if her familiar was loud in class? What if her familiar was super smelly? What if her familiar ate her homework every day?

The hallway started to feel like a tunnel of doom. Marina wanted to pause time. Right here, right now. Before all her worst nightmares were realized.

But the mayor's voice rang out. "Quick, everyone! Outside! The familiars are coming!"

2

THE FAMILIAR MARINA NEVER SAW COMING

The sunshine was like a spotlight. The seaside sands of Seaside Sands were the stage, and all the ten-year-olds were actors.

The people of three towns gathered in a huge crowd, away from the beach. Onlookers were allowed to watch from a distance, with binoculars. With them were familiars of all species, shapes, and sizes. Once you were bonded, your familiar was always by your side.

Marina tried to find her dad and brother (and Crabby and Sea Lion) in the crowd, but she couldn't see them.

"Welcome to Pairing Day! I am Mayor Meilleure Mejor, mayor of Seaside Sands. Thank you for joining us, Riverside Reeds and Woodside Timbers! And now . . . the sun is at its highest point!"

The audience around the kids cheered.

Nothing happened. Was something supposed to happen?

Marina tried to remember how the pairings started when Harbor was getting his sea lion three years ago. She wished Harbor was with her now. He always made her feel better because he never worried about anything.

The ground shook. Marina looked up and saw . . . a stampede!

Elephants, lions, giraffes from the southwest. Turkeys, pigs, sheep from the northwest. Bears, deer, raccoons from the north. Alligators, frogs, beavers from the south. Very wriggly bugs popped up from the ground.

There were cats, dogs, bunnies, ferrets, mice, hamsters, and hedgehogs. Birds, bats, and flying squirrels

were swooping down from the sky. Dolphins, sting-rays, sharks, lobsters, seahorses, and turtles rode in on the tide.

Turtle!

Marina turned to a cluster of three turtles. They waddled her way. She threw her arms wide, and—

They walked past her. One of the turtles crawled onto Wade's foot and nibbled at his toe.

"Aww, buddy!" Wade said, picking up his turtle.

And they were bonded. Marina didn't know *how* she knew. She just knew.

It was a zoo. Animals swirled around like a whirl-pool. Meanwhile, Marina continued to worry.

Mayor Mejor had said that a familiar would come to her . . . but Marina found it impossible to wait. She tried to move closer, but animals were dodging and ducking around her. Every time Marina got near an animal, it ran away. She felt like she was wearing familiar repellent. What if her familiar got lost? What if it was at a different Pairing Day ceremony, looking for her just as frantically as she was looking for it?

To her left, a girl bonded with an eel. To her right, a boy bonded with a butterfly. Someone Marina knew from her lower-school class was petting her new pygmy goat.

The blond boy that had sat in front of Marina was trying to calm his new hippo. Marina didn't see the

girl with black hair in a short, sharp haircut.

There were a group of kids from a neighboring town with a monkey, flamingo, French bulldog, zebra, and wombat.

It seemed like almost everyone had made their bond, but not Marina. She was still chasing animals. She rushed toward a cluster of hermit crabs, who scattered away. What if her familiar didn't like her? What if that's why it was delayed?

At the edge of the beach, a sloth was crawling toward everyone.

Of course, Marina thought. *My familiar is just very, very slow. That explains everything.* One step, two step. The sloth was painfully sluggish.

It stopped at the foot of a kid named Remy, also from Marina's class.

"Finally!" Remy said as the sloth wrapped itself around their body. "You found me! You're slower than a snail. I'll call you Snail."

Marina looked around for her own sloth, or snail,

or very, very, very, very, *very* slow slug. Nothing came.

She felt ill, watching all the familiars cuddle with their human pairs.

The animals were leaving now. The land animals went marching home. The sea creatures slipped back into the ocean, not to be seen again until next year, when they would try to find a match. Every human had an animal pairing, but the reverse was not true. Some animals would never bond with a human.

What if . . .

What if she was like those rudderless animals? What if she was the only person in the world without a familiar?

Marina was numb. She worried about everything all the time. But she never dreamed that *this* could happen. It was the familiar she never saw coming . . . because her familiar never came.

"Excellent!" Mayor Mejor said as Peckadilly pecked her head. "Now that everyone has their familiar, we can head to the Pairing Day celebrat—"

Marina raised her hand. "I don't."

"What?"

She felt sick to her stomach. "I don't have a familiar," Marina said, louder.

Every eye—from all three towns—stared at her.

UNPRECEDENTED

"This is unprecedented!" Mayor Mejor said. "Just . . . unprecedented!"

"Are you sure it's not a lice?" said the boy next to her, with his bluebird. "Those are small and hard to see."

"'Lice' is plural. Singular is 'louse,'" someone corrected. Then they shouted at Marina, "Are you sure you don't have a louse?"

"Or a mouse?"

"Or a grouse!"

"Or a frog?"

"Or a dog?"

"Or a hog!"

"This is unprecedented!" Mayor Mejor said again.

"I don't have one either!" said a loud voice from across the sand. It was the girl with light brown skin and short black hair, who had been sitting in front of Marina. The one who said she'd rather die than have a woodpecker.

She'd probably prefer a woodpecker over this, Marina thought miserably.

The girl marched over to Marina. She was frowning, and her arms were folded.

"Two! *Two!* This has never—this is *unprecedented.*"

Marina wished she knew what that meant.

At first, everyone seemed curious. Now they seemed afraid of them. They stepped away, so that Marina and the other girl were standing alone.

"At least we're together," the girl said to Marina. Those four words made Marina feel so warm inside.

So thankful. "I'm Kit from Woodside Timbers."

"Marina. From here . . . Seaside Sands."

"Anyone else?" Mayor Mejor called. "Anyone else not have a familiar?"

There was silence.

Then everyone took another step away from Marina and Kit. Like they had a contagious disease.

"Congratulations to, uh, almost everyone. It's time to head to the celebration party, in the public library and its courtyard. Humans, please make sure your familiars do not eat the books. I assure you, the cookbooks do not taste like their pictures." People began to shuffle toward the library. Marina and Kit too. Then the mayor dropped her voice and said, "Not you two. You wait here. I—I need to look something up . . . make some calls. Unprecedented!"

Were they in trouble? What if they were kicked out of their hometowns? Marina's insides twisted as she watched the mayor scurry away and disappear inside city hall.

Kit waded into the ocean. The water was up to her knees. Marina started to follow but stopped short, at ankle-deep. Swimming had never come easy to her, like it did for Dad and Harbor. She always felt like she was fighting the ocean, struggling against every wave. And with every stroke, she overthought: the creatures, the riptides, the depth of the ocean, the width of the ocean, the unknowing of everything lurking beneath her, the dread that she could slip under so quietly and easily . . .

Kit didn't seem to have those same worries. She kicked the waves casually. "I hope this means our families got our birthdays wrong. Maybe we're only nine, and our true Pairing Day is *next* year."

"Maybe," Marina said. She wanted Kit's idea to be true, even though she knew it wasn't. "I really wanted a sea creature."

"Yeah?" Kit seemed interested. "Like a narwhal? They *are* the unicorns of the sea."

"Not a narwhal. Something real."

"Narwhals are totally real, Marina!"

"I've lived by the sea my whole life, and I've never ever seen a narwhal."

"So?" Kit said. "I haven't seen a tiger. Are tigers not real?" Kit smirked like she'd caught Marina in a trap.

The wind blew. The townspeople were gone. From across the beach, figures were heading toward them. The mayor?

No, it was just Marina's family and Kit's grandparents. Marina's dad had tried to hide his crab familiar in his shirt, so that Marina didn't feel bad. But Crabby ended up pinching her dad on his chest.

"Don't worry—*ouch!*—Marina. It will—*ouch!*—all be okay."

"I'll share Sea Lion with you," Harbor said. "I really will." Sea Lion scooted over to Marina and planted a sloppy kiss on her kneecap.

It was a kind but gross gesture.

Kit's grandparents rubbed her back. They both had salamanders or newts or geckos on their shoulders. Marina couldn't really tell the difference.

"This is a mistake," her grandmother said. "We will sort this out."

"How long do we have to wait, anyway?" Kit asked, bored. "I want to go home."

"You're not going home without a familiar!" Kit's grandmother said. "And I'm not going home until we find out who stole yours."

They waited forever on the sandy seaside of Seaside Sands. Kit's grandmother checked her watch often and clucked her tongue in disapproval. Kit and her grandfather began collecting seashells in a neat pile. Harbor threw a ball for Sea Lion to fetch over and over . . . until Sea Lion got bored and began splashing around in the ocean. Marina and her father played too many rounds of tic-tac-toe in the sand.

Soon, the sun was no longer above their heads. It was halfway across the sky. The light twinkled on the surface of the water. The afternoon was breezy.

At last, many shadows appeared across the beach—Mayor Mejor in front, with her woodpecker hammering her hair. Behind her were a bunch of kids and a handful of adults. Marina didn't recognize any of them. They definitely weren't from Seaside Sands.

"What is this?" Kit's grandmother demanded. "Where did you disappear to, Mayor? Why did you take so long?"

"Quickly, this way," the mayor said, ushering three girls into a circle with Marina and Kit. "Now put your hands in the middle."

Marina held out her hand.

Kit shrugged and did the same.

A short, plump, freckled blond girl in glasses put out her hand.

So did a pale, redheaded girl with hair shorter than Harbor's.

And last, a tall, pigtailed girl with dark brown skin held out her only hand—her right one.

At once, their palms began to glow. A soft light surrounded them all.

"What's happening?" Marina whispered.

"We're radioactive!" laughed the redhead.

The mayor was delighted. "Like I said . . . unprecedented."

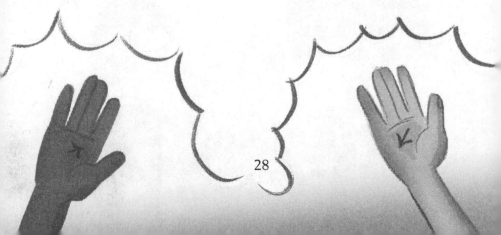

WHERE THE ARROWS POINT

Marina broke away first. Hands were *not* supposed to glow like this. She tried to rub the glow off.

Kit's eyes gleamed. "I think this means we're special."

"I don't want to be special," Marina mumbled. "I want to be like everyone else."

"Yawn," Kit said. "How boring!"

The blond girl sat down on the sand and looked dreamily out into the water. "That would be very sad indeed. You'd lose the unique things that make you *you*."

Kit's eyes widened. "Scratch that! I'm stealing her answer!" Then she turned to the girl on the ground. "What's your name?"

"Pippa," she said. Then she started to hum to herself as she drew flowers in the sand.

The tall girl was still examining her hand. "There's an arrow! On my palm! But . . ." She compared her hand to the redheaded girl next to her. "Mine is pointing in a different direction from Hailey's."

The redhead—Hailey—grinned. "Ha! Well, what are we waiting for, Ember? Adventure calls! We have to follow it now!"

"But where does it lead?" the girl named Ember said.

"To your familiars," Mayor Mejor answered, her eyes bright.

Kit sighed and folded her arms. "We have to go fetch our familiars? I thought they were supposed to come to us!"

"Not for the Mythics."

"The *what?*"

Marina looked around at her dad and brother, but they looked just as confused as she felt. None of the kids—and none of their families—knew what a Mythic was.

The mayor smiled. "Let me back up. First, I apologize for disappearing on you," she said to Marina and Kit. "I needed to call the other regions to see if this phenomenon happened in their Pairing Day ceremonies too."

"You didn't get familiars either?" Marina asked.

Ember shook her head sadly.

"First, I called Lavaside Rocks, Mountainside Snows, and Tundraside Frosts," Mayor Mejor said. "I know those three share a Pairing Day. But no luck . . . Their ceremonies went off without a hitch. Then I called the cluster of Desertside Dunes, Savannaside Grasses, and Jungleside Vines, but again, no dice. I began to give up hope that the other three Mythics would present themselves. But then!" Mayor Mejor clapped excitedly, and Peckadilly jabbed her beehive with increased speed. "When I called Prairieside Meadows, Cliffside Ledges, and Splashside Falls—"

"I was just about to call *you* when you called me," squeaked a tiny man who looked as old as time itself. "I'm Mayor Verioldman of Cliffside Ledges. Of which Hailey and Ember are residents. Yes, there are *two* Mythics from my town," he boasted as his tarsier familiar stared unblinkingly at Marina.

"And last, I called Waterside Isles, Swampside Shrubs, and Lakeside Muds."

"That's my town!" Pippa said, looking up from her doodles in the sand. "Lakeside Muds."

A reedy, no-nonsense woman named Mayor Loch introduced herself as the Lakeside Muds mayor. A poison dart frog sat atop her head. "Well. Never in my life did I think I'd live to see this. This is a very"—she hesitated, searching for the right word—"*surprising* turn of events."

"Let me explain," Mayor Mejor said.

"Well, someone should!" Kit grumbled.

"I first heard about the legend of the Mythics from the mayor before me, who heard it from the mayor before him. It's a story long passed down from mayor to mayor in every town. Long ago, the Mythics protected the world. Their familiars are powerful mythical beasts, and the Mythics use these mighty familiars to keep everyone safe. They appear in this world when there is trouble brewing."

Ember frowned. "What kind of trouble?"

"A disturbance in the peace."

"That's all you can say?" Kit said.

"That's all I know. If the trouble was in Seaside Sands, I'd tell you, but it's not here. And I don't know where it could be."

"Me neither!" Mayor Verioldman squeaked.

Mayor Loch nodded.

"We wish we could help more," Mayor Mejor said, "but this is a journey you must take on your own. First, you're going to have to find your familiars. Then you're going to have to locate the trouble. And once you do, fight it. It's up to you to save the world."

Marina had a stomachache. Her stomachache had a stomachache. Her stomachache's stomachache had a stomachache.

No way, no way, *no way* was she going to fight trouble or save the world. This must be a mistake.

She was the wrong person for this.

"Are you okay?" Pippa asked, looking up at Marina from the sand.

Marina shook her head no.

Mayor Mejor kept talking. "The Mythics have special familiars . . . unlike any other. Your familiars are called Mythies. They are mythical creatures thought not to be real."

Marina gasped. "Like a narwhal?"

"Narwhals are real, Marina! Like I told you before!" Kit said.

The mayor continued, "You have to earn your familiar. In quests of courage."

"This. Is. AWESOME," Hailey squealed.

"And we're supposed to go together?" Ember asked.

"The Mythics *are* a team."

Marina looked around. She suddenly felt like a weak link. But Ember stared right at Marina when she said, "We can do this."

"And can we bring our families?" Pippa said, looking at hers hopefully.

"Unfortunately not," Mayor Loch said, her frog leaping from her head. She plucked it off the ground before it hopped away. "You have no idea how much power you're about to obtain. The Mythics and their Mythies are the only ones who can manage the journey ahead."

Hailey was bouncing. "I hope we get to sword-fight. Swashbuckle. Swishventure."

"What was that last one?" Kit laughed.

Marina was not laughing. Suddenly she was

expected to leave home? Go adventuring across the world? It sounded like someone else's life. She looked to her dad and brother in panic. If only they were as scared as she felt . . . but they weren't. They seemed excited for her.

Please forbid me from going, Marina thought. She was desperate. *Please stop me. Please ground me. Please read my mind.*

"I think you should go," Dad said.

Marina sighed. Oh, the betrayal!

Marina tried again to rub the glow off her hand. She wiped her palm on her pants. Then she went into the ocean and tried to wash it off. No matter what she did, her hand would not stop blazing with light.

Stupid hand, she thought, staring at it.

"Let me see," Ember said earnestly. She looked at Marina's palm. "Your arrow is brighter than mine. See how dazzling yours is?"

"What does that mean?"

"I'm not sure," Ember said. "Pippa, can I see your hand?"

Pippa held out her palm. Her arrow was glowing even fainter than Ember's. When Hailey and Kit saw everyone comparing arrows, they offered their hands too.

No doubt about it, Marina's arrow was brighter than the other arrows.

What is wrong with me? Marina thought. Even among misfits, she was the biggest misfit to ever not fit!

"It's pointing into the sea," Kit observed. "Just like you wanted."

Marina had wanted a sea creature . . . but not like this!

"We should follow the brightest arrow first," Ember said.

Pippa traced her fingers across Marina's arrow, reading her palm. "I agree."

"I think it will be good to get Marina's Mythie

first," Kit said. "The longer we wait, the more time you have to get nervous, Marina."

"Then it's settled!" Hailey said. "We have to steal a pirate ship!"

"Or . . . I could just give you my mayoral boat," Mayor Mejor said. "After all, what is the SS *Seashanty* good for, if not times like these?"

"Aw." Hailey pouted. "That's no fun."

"That would be excellent, Mayor Mejor," Ember said. "Thank you very much!"

The Mythics and their families all wandered into

town to purchase supplies. Since the rest of Seaside Sands was at the Pairing Day party, the streets and shops were empty. All three mayors paid for the supplies, writing a note to each shopkeeper and leaving money behind.

The girls, their families, and the three mayors carried crates of water and food to the boat: many boxes of tinned fish because that was what Seaside Sands was known for. The whole town revolved around the sea.

But Marina's dad, an experienced fishing-boat captain, made them pack a crateful of imported fruits and vegetables, as well as granola, juice boxes, and chocolate. "I love fish, but you can't live off fish alone," he said.

They stopped at a pharmacy and got multivitamins, as requested by Kit's grandparents. They also got medicine, gauze, and bandages, as requested by Hailey's mom and stepdad.

Then they went to a clothing shop, since the girls

were in for a long journey ahead. Marina grabbed enough items for everybody: sleeping bags, socks, extra sneakers, and hats to shield their faces from the sun.

Arms full of the most useful, practical items, Marina looked over at Hailey. Hailey was admiring herself in the mirror. She wore a vest, a bandanna, a shark's-tooth necklace, and an eyepatch.

"Ahoy!" Hailey said, brandishing a plastic play sword before heading to the register with the stuff.

Marina shook her head.

By the time the ship was fully stocked, the citizens of Seaside Sands were leaving the Pairing Day celebration. The streets were filled with humans

and animals in party hats. The Woodside Timbers people were climbing into the deer-and-moose-pulled wagons that were going to take them home. The Riverside Reeds folks were getting into boats that were steered and guided by aquatic familiars. Familiar-travel was faster than any other form of transportation. Marina knew that the magic of familiars and the strength of their bonds caused a multiplication of speed and energy that took a vehicle to its destination in half the time—or faster.

Now that everyone else was leaving, it was time for the Mythics to depart too. Marina knew it. But she didn't want to embrace it. She wanted to cling to this moment—with her dad and her brother, safe in her hometown—forever. But time cruelly marched on.

"We're ready," Ember said. "Let's do this! Let's go get our familiars."

Kit wore a sly smile. "Starting with Marina's non-narwhal!"

"Are you okay, Marina?" Pippa asked. "You're looking a little blue."

Was she okay? So much was changing, so fast. Marina didn't like change. It made her queasy.

She smiled. Well, she tried to smile. It was more like a wince. "I'm okay . . . I think."

"Then off you go," Mayor Mejor said, handing them the keys to the SS *Seashanty*.

5

THE WARNING

The goodbyes were way too short.

Kit's grandparents nagged her to take her morning vitamins and mind her manners. Kit rolled her eyes.

Ember's mothers reminded her to have faith in herself and always trust her gut.

"You are brave. You are strong," they told her. Ember nodded.

Pippa's family tackled her with hugs and kisses. She was the second oldest of seven kids. She laughed as her siblings planted kisses on her round cheeks.

"Don't forget us!" the youngest cried.

"How could I forget my very heart?" Pippa said.

Hailey's mom, stepdad, older sister, and younger sister told her to be patient. And thoughtful. "Please don't dive into danger," her older sister begged.

"Promise," Hailey said. Her fingers were crossed behind her back.

And then there was Marina's family.

"This adventure will be good for you," her dad said.

"In what way?" Marina asked. "I don't want to leave home!"

"Home will always be waiting for you when you return."

"But home is where you and Harbor are."

"Home will always be when we are together," Dad agreed. "But growth happens when you go somewhere new."

"Besides, the other Mythics need you," Harbor added. "You are really smart."

"Did you just compliment your sister?" Dad asked.

"Don't worry. It will never happen again."

Marina laughed through her tears. "Okay." She sniffed. "But when I get my Mythie, I'm coming back."

"You better," Dad said. He kissed Marina's head, and Crabby pinched her nose.

Every Mythic walked onto the gangway, waving goodbye to the loved ones behind them.

Don't think about all the ways this could go wrong, Marina thought.

So, of course, it was *all* Marina could think about.

Boats sinking. Cyclone storms. Hungry sharks. Hidden shallow shelves. Rip currents. Lightning. Tsunamis. Sunburns. Seasickness. Dehydration. Starvation. Sharks. Jellyfish. Stonefish. Regular fish . . . hey, you never knew.

"You coming, Marina?" Pippa asked, putting a gentle hand on her back.

"Mmm."

Marina looked at the mayor, who looked as green as algae.

"Before you go, I should tell you about the—"

"What?" Marina shouted. The wind was howling. She barely heard what the mayor had said.

Mayor Mejor gulped. "You know what? It's probably nothing."

"Hurry up, you two!" Ember called from the ship's steering wheel.

"Yeah, Captain Ember has chores for us all. Get scrubbing, deckhand!" Kit teased.

"Come on," Pippa said, tenderly touching Marina's arm. "Everyone's waiting for us."

Marina looked at the boat. The Mythics were ready to go. But then she turned back to the mayor, and . . . Mayor Mejor was pacing on the dock. Marina recognized the nauseated expression on her face. The mayor was nervous about something, and Marina was the only one who noticed.

"You go on ahead, Pippa. I'll catch up," Marina said. Then she walked down the gangway. The mayor was biting her nails. That was never a good sign. "Mayor?" Marina said. "What's wrong?"

"Just . . . I don't want to spoil your perfect day."

"This is *not* a perfect day for me. There's nothing to spoil," Marina said.

The mayor frowned. "At first, I didn't want to

say anything in front of your families, in case they forbade you from going. And then . . . you girls seemed so excited that I didn't have the heart to tell you . . ."

"Tell us what?"

Mayor Mejor took a deep breath. "There are going to be people after you. Well, they'll be after your Mythies. There are some people in Terrafamiliar who will do *anything* to get their hands on that kind of raw power. Please be careful. You are all in grave danger."

See, it was exactly sentences like that that made Marina despise adventures!

Marina walked up the gangway like she was walking the plank. She tried one last time to scrub the arrow off her hand. This was the arrow of *ruin*!

All too soon, she was on the boat. Kit started the motor, and Ember steered the boat away from the dock. Their families waved and shouted. Pippa blew kisses from the side, while Hailey ran up and down the deck. Gloomily, Marina watched her dad and Harbor until they were specks in the distance.

Then the shoreline disappeared behind them. There was no turning back now.

See What We Could See Sea See

Right away, they had a big problem. Once the water grew choppy, it was time to open the mainsail, and Marina gasped in horror. The boat's sail looked like a piece of Swiss cheese. Peckadilly must have hammered it to death. And the woodpecker didn't stop at the mainsail or jib—it drilled the deck and the sides too. With all the holes, it was truly a miracle that the SS *Seashanty* didn't sink.

Pippa and Hailey got to work patching up the boat. They tried stuffing all the holes with socks. They were so enthusiastic about the job that Marina

didn't have the heart to tell them it wouldn't make a difference.

The open sea stretched before them. The waves rocked the ship gently. It was like a baby's cradle. Marina liked the way it swayed. As much as she hated swimming, she had always liked boats—ever since she was a toddler, and her mom and dad used to take her and Harbor sailing. Her parents had even let her steer the boat sometimes.

She wondered what her mom would think of all this Mythics business. She wished she could talk to her. Her mom was the only person who could make her worries go away. After her mom had died three years ago, the worries never went away again. They were there permanently, like a roommate but worse.

The boat dipped again, and a groan echoed from the starboard side. Kit wasn't doing so well with the movement. She was looking very sweaty.

"I can't believe they gave us the keys to a boat!" Hailey giggled as she hung upside down off the yard-arm. "They know we're ten years old, right?"

"Hailey, be careful!" Ember said.

"I do not know what that word means," Hailey said. And she cackled maniacally.

"Marina, I need to see your hand," Ember said. Marina crossed the deck and held out her palm. As the ship voyaged farther into the ocean, Marina's

arrow grew brighter and brighter. It was like a compass on her palm, pointing due familiar.

"They just let us go!" Hailey marveled. "I can't believe this is happening to me. To us!"

"Yes, this is just *great*," Kit said as she crouched over a bucket.

"It's going to be okay," Pippa said, standing beside her.

"You should leave," Kit warned her.

"Why?"

"Because I'm about to hurl again. You don't have to be here, Pippa."

"I know. But I want to be."

Kit gave her a watery smile . . . before face-planting in her bucket again. Pippa gently rubbed Kit's back.

"BEWARE! ICEBERG!" Hailey shouted from above them.

"Hailey, we're in warm waters!" Marina said.

Hailey cackled again. She was an agent of chaos.

Ember turned to Marina. She whispered in a low

voice, "Do you think we'll have to dive deep into the ocean to get your familiar?"

Marina frowned. "There's only so far we can go. In very, very deep water, there is something called water pressure. It's when all the water above you puts weight on your body. It can crush us!"

Ember blinked. "You're very smart, Marina."

"I'm very careful. Sometimes it's the same thing."

Ember seemed like she was thinking about it. But also like she wasn't sure she agreed.

She didn't argue, though. Ember squinted into the horizon.

Suddenly, the wheel began to spin. Ember pushed against it with her right hand and her left arm to keep the wheel from turning.

"Marina, can you help me? It feels stuck!"

Marina grabbed the other side. She pulled while Ember pushed, and eventually the wheel stopped resisting.

"Thanks," Ember said. "That wheel was super heavy, and I did *not* have a good grip on it."

Marina looked down at Ember's arm. She had a million questions.

"I was born this way," Ember explained, following Marina's line of sight.

"Is it hard to only have one hand?" Marina asked.

"Yes and no," Ember said. "Some tasks can be difficult, like shoelaces, buttons, zippers, opening wrappers, putting my hair up. But I've been doing these things all my life, and I've learned how to take care of myself. Or ask for help when I need it."

"Well, you can always come to me," Marina offered.

"Thanks," Ember said. "But I like to try to work things out on my own first. My moms always taught me grit and resilience."

"My mom tried to teach me the same thing . . ." Marina winced. "I'm not sure the lesson stuck, though."

They sailed on. The wind was fierce. The sun had dipped below the horizon line; only echoes of sunlight were in the sky now. It was getting cold.

Marina couldn't believe this was where her day was ending. When she had woken up this morning, she'd thought she was going to get her familiar, go to a party, then go back to her regular life. And now she was on a ship in the middle of the ocean, looking for an imaginary animal.

"Marina . . . can you handle the wheel alone for a second?"

Marina took over. Ember walked to the side of the ship and looked through a handheld telescope. She frowned.

Marina knew that expression all too well.

It was worry.

"What's wrong?" Marina asked.

"There's a boat following us."

Marina took a deep breath. Don't think about the worst-case scenario. But of course, then she could *only* think of the worst-case scenario.

Monsters. Pirates. Monster pirates.

"Is it Mayor Mejor?" Hailey asked, climbing down the mast.

"How could it be if we took her boat?" Ember said.

"Our families?" Kit said. "My grandparents are so overprotective. They would totally follow."

Ember frowned. "Maybe."

Or maybe not.

Marina gulped. "The mayor gave me a warning," she admitted, "just before I boarded the ship. She said that people would be following us to try to steal our Mythies. And we're in danger."

Kit moaned. "Was she going to tell anyone *else* this extremely important information?"

"She almost didn't even tell me. Maybe whoever's following us . . ." Marina didn't have to finish the sentence.

Ember exchanged a look with Marina. A look

that asked: *What do we do?*

"Me?" Marina whispered.

Ember nodded.

"Whoever it is, they're gaining fast!" Hailey said.

Right. Marina had to act. She took a deep, shivery breath. "Ember, keep watching with the spyglass. Hailey, we're tacking, so beware of the boom."

"Excellent!" Hailey said. "And that means?"

"Duck!"

Hailey bent down as the sail came swinging toward her. It narrowly missed her head.

"Great. Now, Kit—"

Kit looked up at her with a nauseated expression.

"Uh . . . stay by your bucket."

Kit hugged the bucket tighter. It was her sea version of a comfort blanket.

"Pippa! Yank the motor!"

"Aye aye, Captain!" Pippa said with a warm smile. "I knew you could do it, Marina."

Marina laughed nervously. "Enough chatter, landlubbers! Full steam ahead!"

NO SOCKS!

The Mythics sped merrily along. At last, the boat behind them disappeared. Marina might have felt better . . . if they weren't so far out in the middle of the sea. She continued to steer the ship. She was following her arrow. But where was her arrow going?

All traces of sunlight were gone now. The ocean was an endless dark expanse. The stars were like freckles in the sky. Hailey and Ember stayed by Marina's side, keeping her company. Kit was still in the same spot she always was, occasionally moaning. And it wasn't until Pippa came climbing up from the lower deck of the boat that Marina even realized she had disappeared for a spell.

"Everyone?" Pippa said. Her shoes squeaked as she walked, and she trailed water behind her. When Pippa reached Marina, Hailey, and Ember, she dropped a large wooden box. It hit the deck with a *kerplunk*. "I have good news. The bottom of the boat is flooding. This is the only food box I could save. Oh, and I think we're going to sink."

"Pippa, that's *bad* news," Marina said.

"I know," she said mournfully. "I just wanted to make you feel good before I brought you down."

"The boat is sinking?!" Ember cried, jumping to her feet.

"I have to watch you drown?!" Hailey shouted.

"We're *all* drowning at the same time!" Kit yelled from across the boat.

"No, I'm drowning last! I can hold my breath for two minutes and forty-six seconds!"

"This is bad!" Ember said. "How much water is down there?"

"It was up to my ankles."

The boat bobbed over a particularly large wave, and Kit groaned.

Ember was pacing across the deck. "This is so, so, so bad! How do we fix a flood?"

"There's no fixing it!" Hailey said, running to the edge of the boat. "We all have to jump overboard. Escape the boat."

Kit hugged her bucket. "This is a nightmare. You're tucked in bed, safe and sound in Woodside Timbers. Wake up, Kit!"

"Three," Hailey bellowed. "Two—"

"STOP!" Marina shouted. She had to take charge.

There was too much panic, even for her. There was a problem; she had to solve it. She had to *think* . . .

"We have to find the hole! And we have to plug it up."

"GRAB THE SOCKS!" Hailey shouted.

"No socks!" Marina said. "Socks will only absorb water. First things first—let's find the leak!"

Marina, Hailey, Pippa, and Ember scurried down the ladder into freezing-cold seawater that was now knee-high.

"This is bad! So bad! So very bad!" Marina whimpered.

The lights were flickering. Marina calculated that they had fifteen minutes—maybe less—before the water would be up to their necks. After that, the boat would capsize completely, and . . . well, Marina didn't want to think about what happened after that.

"I want to help," Pippa said, shivering in the cold water. "What can I do?"

"Go find the problem spot! Ember, go with her!" They waded away, down the hall, toward the kitchen and the bathroom.

"What about me?" Hailey said.

"You're quick and energetic—help me find things to seal the hole!"

Hailey and Marina shuffled toward a storage closet. Hailey began to grab everything in sight: a hat, a flashlight, a fishing hook, sunscreen.

"Um, Hailey, we need to find things that will plug up a hole, remember?"

"I know," she said. "I just want this stuff for later—ooh! Some fireworks!"

"There won't *be* a later if we don't get the hole patched!" Marina said.

This was not working. She couldn't even hear Pippa or Ember anymore—were they having any luck? Marina had to go find them. She turned back around to grab Hailey. In the flickering light, Hailey was grabbing socks.

"No socks!" Marina groaned.

"But these have funky little anchors on them!" Hailey said, slipping them on her hands like mittens.

Marina pulled Hailey away from the closet. The water was up to their thighs. They were in serious trouble. Arms linked, they pushed through. It was a struggle. They passed Mayor Mejor's tiny bedroom, but no one was inside. They passed the kitchen—again, empty.

They found Ember and Pippa squeezed into the bathroom. They were under the water. The lights flickered violently.

Almost instantly, Pippa came up for air, gasping.

"What are you doing?" Marina said.

"We think the hole is over here! We followed the current, but . . ." Pippa wiped off her glasses, which were dripping wet. "I can't see under there."

Marina was just about to ask whether her glasses were getting in the way when Kit's voice echoed down from the deck above. "Um . . . Marina? We've got a problem!"

"Another one?!"

"The mystery boat from earlier—it's back!"

There were too many problems . . . Marina couldn't handle them all! Her heart pounded, and her breath raced. They had five minutes left, if that. She looked at the arrow on her palm. If ever there was a time for a Mythie to save them . . .

But a Mythie didn't come.

Marina was at the helm. *She* had to save herself.

Think . . . Think . . .

At last, Ember came up for air. She spluttered and coughed up water. "It's pitch-black! How are we supposed to see anything down there?"

The lights flashed again. If only the light would stay on. What they needed was . . .

"Light!" Marina said, turning to Hailey. A sudden, mad burst of inspiration flooded her. "You took the flashlight from the supply closet!"

"Oh, have you come to Hailey's cabinet of curios?" Hailey said, opening her vest and revealing all sorts of objects in her inner pockets. "*This* is what you seek!" She turned the flashlight on, then brandished it like a sword. "Unless you'd like the socks?"

"No socks!" Marina said.

"Just checking!"

"Marina!" Kit cried from above. "It's following us!"

Marina took a deep breath. One job at a time, one problem at a time. They could find the hole, but they still had nothing to plug it with. "Pippa," Marina said, her voice rising as rapidly as the water. "I bet you were paying attention to the items in each room. Go find something to stuff the hole with! And no socks!"

Pippa nodded and disappeared.

The boat lurched, and water splashed Marina's face. The lights sputtered like a dying engine. Marina knew they were minutes away from the electricity being flooded, which meant no lights, and worst of all—*no motor*. They wouldn't be able to outrun the boat behind them.

One problem at a time, she reminded herself. "Let's go!" she said, and she dove underwater with Ember and Hailey. The salt stung her eyes, but the flashlight proved useful. They spotted the hole: fist-sized, in the corner.

When they came up for air, Pippa was in the doorway. "I found the perfect thing to plug the leak," she panted. "But it's on the top shelf. I can't reach—I'm too short!"

They all looked to the tallest Mythic.

"On it!" said Ember, swimming out of the room.

Ember and Pippa didn't take long at all, but with water rising from their thighs to their shoulders . . . it felt like forever.

High above her head, Ember was carrying a tarp and a small pillow. "One of these?" she cried.

The hole was too deep now to really know which one would be best. Marina calculated as quick

as she could. The tarp was water-proof but not very expandable. The pillow was expandable but not very waterproof.

"Both!" Marina said. Ember tossed her the objects, and Marina wrapped the pillow in the waterproof tarp.

"Hailey," Marina said, the water up to her neck. Pippa had stopped being able to touch ground completely. She was treading water. "Two minutes and forty-six seconds."

Hailey grinned and took the tarp-wrapped pillow from Marina. "Watch me." Hailey took an enormous breath and dove down. Marina followed her under, holding the flashlight steady as Hailey—the record holder for breath-holding—stuffed the pillow into the hole.

But it wouldn't stick. The pressure from the water pushed the pillow back in the boat. Marina wanted to scream—or at least curse Peckadilly for all eternity.

She came up for air. Hailey didn't.

"What's going on?" Ember said.

"Pillow keeps wiggling out!"

The water was up to her mouth now. She had to tilt her head up if she wanted air. This was it—they were absolutely going to sink in the ocean. She wondered if Dad and Harbor would regret sending her on this adventure *now*.

Hailey popped up from the water. "*You*," she said, swimming toward Marina, "owe me an apology!"

They were going to drown, and Hailey wanted an *apology*? Was she serious?! "For what?" Marina spluttered.

Hailey grinned. She lifted up her hands . . . her *bare* hands.

"You . . . what? I don't understand," Ember said, looking between Marina and Hailey confusedly.

"The pillow was too big for the hole. That's why it kept popping out. So I tied the pillow tighter. YES, SOCKS!"

Marina laughed. She laughed so hard she started crying, which—mixed with the seawater on her lips—tasted very salty. It was all so relieving . . . so funny.

Until the lights sizzled. And died.

"Marina!" Kit shouted from the deck. "Help!"

THE PROMISE

Marina swam, looking for the ladder and feeling her way through the hull. Pippa, Hailey, and Ember were right behind her. None of them could see at all. But now that the below-deck problem was solved, they had to help Kit above deck. The mystery boat was probably so close by now.

Her hands closed around rungs—the ladder! Marina pulled herself up as quickly as she could, trying not to shiver in her wet clothes.

"Finally!" Kit said when Marina reached the deck. "Look behind us!"

Marina turned to the stern and finally saw what Kit was seeing: A tiny boat with a single white headlight. It was clearly in their wake.

What could they possibly do?

The victory below deck was short-lived; that anxious feeling was creeping up in her again. What did she always do when she was scared? Run or hide.

Running was impossible. The ship was waterlogged. It would be sluggish until they got the water out of the hull. They couldn't use the motor anyway because the electricity had short-circuited. They were completely without power, which left them powerless.

Hiding was laughable. It wasn't like she could hide a big boat like this! Unless . . .

When they were in the bathroom below and the lights flickered out, Marina couldn't see *anything*. None of them could. The ship lights were already extinguished, thanks to the water. But above deck, there were lanterns lit—ones that weren't connected to the ship.

"Turn all the lights off!" Marina said. "Quickly!"

"Why?" Kit asked, clicking off the lamp next to her.

"Because if we can't outrun this mystery ship, then we have to outsmart them. We're going full chameleon."

The Mythics scurried around the ship, extinguishing every gas lamp and battery lamp. With the lights off both inside and outside the boat, they blended in with the dark of night and the dark of the ocean.

The five Mythics hung over the stern of the SS

Seashanty, watching as the mystery boat swerved from left to right—looking for something, looking for them. After a while, it chose a direction and sailed . . .

The wrong direction.

They sighed in relief, Marina loudest of all.

"It worked! Your plan worked! You genius!" Ember said, squeezing her tight.

"Seriously—your Mythie better be one giant brain," Kit said.

"Let's celebrate with a party!" Hailey said.

"And a nap," Pippa added.

"Well . . ." Marina grimaced, but no one could see it in the darkness. "You all are about to hate me. This chameleon plan only works at night. The second the sun comes up, our ship is visible again. And right now, the ship won't go very fast, or anywhere at all, as long as there's all that water inside."

Kit groaned. "Oh no, please don't say it—"

"We have to work together to empty the ship."

"She said it!"

They may not have been happy about it, but Marina, Kit, Pippa, Ember, and Hailey got to work.

They spent *ages* in an assembly line, moving Kit's bucket into the hull, scooping up water, raising it up the ladder, and dumping it over the side. They didn't clear the boat of water—not by a long shot—but they got enough of it out that Marina was confident the electricity would dry out, and the boat could run again.

When they were done, they created a nest of sleeping bags and blankets on the deck. At last, they collapsed in a heap, too tired to move. Marina didn't have a watch, but it must have been two in the morning, at least. Later than she had ever stayed up before. The sky was deep and dark. She was certain there was still enough night left to work in a good sleep. If only she wasn't so hungry. Her stomach growled loudly. So did Ember's.

"Thank goodness Pippa was able to save a box of food," Ember said.

"But what's in it?" Hailey asked suspiciously, sitting up and poking it with her toe.

"I don't know," Pippa said. "I haven't opened it yet. I hope it's the box with cheese and crackers."

Hailey wiggled over to the box and pulled off the lid. She shined the flashlight. "APRICOTS!"

"Dried apricots," Marina said, inspecting the box's contents.

"That's even worse!" Hailey said.

"At least it's *dry* dried apricots," Ember said. "Much better than the wet dried apricots below deck."

"Ugh! How about apri*nots*," Hailey said as she dug deeper into the box. "Oooh! There's something at the bottom! It's—*blech!* Canned fish!"

Marina hummed. "That's also a practical food."

Hailey made a sour face. "Well, you can have my share," she said, pushing a tin of sardines into Marina's hands.

"And mine! I'm not hungry anyway," Kit groaned. "If I never see another boat again, it will be *too soon*. This is my first and last time sailing."

Marina ate way too many dried apricots. She ate far too much tinned fish. They were not a good combination. They were not even good on their own.

All the Mythics picked at the sorry sampling. They washed it down with the juice boxes they, thankfully, had kept on the upper deck.

"This is disgustingly disgusting," Hailey said.

"Come on, Hailey. It's not *that* bad," Ember replied.

"Especially if you pretend," Pippa said brightly. "This prune is . . . a chocolate cake. And these sardines are . . ."

"Salty fish?" Kit said with a smirk.

"Imaginary spaghetti!" Pippa said. "Yum!"

Marina smiled. It was odd—this morning, they were strangers. They *still* were strangers. And yet, somehow, Marina felt like she had known them all her life. Perhaps saving a sinking ship had bonded them forever.

And she had to admit . . . the feeling was nice. Until now, Marina didn't know what she was missing. She had never felt *heard* or *seen* by kids her own age before. Back home, she'd tried, but her overthinking often got in the way.

Here, she was just herself. And that was more than enough.

The boat rocked, and the wind blew. As Hailey and Pippa recounted for Kit the story of how they were all nearly swallowed by the sea, Marina looked down at the arrow on her palm. She didn't want to be negative when everyone else was so relieved, but she knew the plug downstairs was just temporary. The hole—and this boat—wouldn't hold out for much longer.

Was her arrow leading them the right way? Even with the other Mythics around her, Marina still felt this gnawing feeling inside of her. Like she was a dried apricot that someone else was chewing.

She swallowed her bite with a gulp. "I'm worried."

"What else is new?" Kit said with a sly smile.

Pippa put a hand on Marina's arm. "What are you thinking about?"

"It's just . . . the ocean is huge. My familiar might be hard to find. What if this boat breaks down before we get to my Mythie? And my arrow may lead us there, but *where* is there? My Mythie might be out of reach. What if it's twenty thousand leagues under the sea? What are the chances it's floating on top of the water?"

"Then we dive deep and get it!" Hailey said. "That's what we're supposed to do, right? Earn our familiars in quests of courage!"

Ember frowned. "Well, that's what I've been wondering. What *are* we supposed to do? We don't seem to have much direction, do we?"

"What do you mean?" Kit asked.

"We have a direction," Hailey said, seizing Marina's hand and examining her palm. "It's . . . that way!"

"Not that kind of direction! I just thought we would get more information before heading out into the open seas," Ember said.

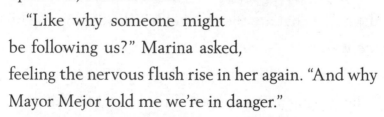

"Like why someone might be following us?" Marina asked, feeling the nervous flush rise in her again. "And why Mayor Mejor told me we're in danger."

Everyone chuckled uneasily. Everyone, that is,

except Hailey, who seemed wholly unconcerned. "Don't worry—I'll protect you!" Hailey said. "My middle name is Danger."

Ember grinned. "I didn't realize 'danger' was spelled G-A-L-E."

"Ember! Don't go spilling my secrets."

"That's what happens when you have two Mythics from the same town."

"Curses!"

"There shouldn't be any secrets between us, anyway," Ember said. "If the Mythics really are a team, then we should act like one."

"Agreed," Marina said. "If we're truly in danger, we're going to need to trust each other and work together. Just like we did today."

"More than that," Pippa added as she squeezed Marina's hand. "We're not *just* a team—we're friends now. That means something."

They all nodded.

Ember said, "Then let's make a promise. Here

and now. To always be honest and true."

"And supportive and kind," Pippa said brightly.

"And brave and courageous and bold and daring!" Hailey added.

"Hailey, you said the same thing four times," Kit pointed out.

"Well, I meant it four times!"

They all looked at Marina, and she gulped. It was her turn, and her mind had gone blank. This was like every public-speaking nightmare she had ever

had. "Uh . . . um . . ."

"Very eloquent," Kit teased.

They were still watching her. Her mouth was dry. She'd been in this position before. In a moment, everyone would get tired of waiting for her to pluck up the nerve to say something, and they'd all move on with the conversation. And she'd have contributed nothing. She could die of embarrassment.

But then . . . the moment passed, and Marina didn't die of embarrassment. And no one moved on without her. Everyone was still waiting. All of a sudden, she realized she actually *hadn't* been in this position before. "We promise," Marina said finally, "to always have each other's backs and to lend a helping hand if one of us is sinking."

"How about when *all* of us are sinking?" Ember said with a wink.

"That ship has already sailed," Marina replied, and everyone laughed.

Kit went last. She smirked. "And we promise

to be significantly less cheesy from here on out." Marina smiled, and Hailey snorted a bit of juice out her nose.

The moon shone bright, and so did their palms. "This we swear," Ember said in a low voice. "Together we are stronger than we are alone. Together we are better than we are apart. Friends forever."

"Friends forever," they agreed.

Like magic, their hearts were bonded together.

"Get some sleep," Ember said. "I'll steer the ship."

"Are you sure?" Marina asked, barely suppressing a yawn.

Ember nodded. "Someone has to."

"But—"

"Sleep, Marina. You might have a quest of courage tomorrow."

"I can switch with you soon," Pippa said. "Wake me in a few hours, Ember."

Under the night sky, they lay in a pile of sleeping bags, blankets, and pillows on the deck of the ship.

Thanks to Peckadilly, the blankets had holes in them, and the stuffing was coming out of all the pillows. The boat gently bobbed. They looked up at the stars.

Marina felt like a star herself—shining and happy. She thought of her mom, but with warmth instead of her usual ache. For years, she had been so certain that bonding with an ocean familiar would

be the best way to honor and remember her mom. But maybe that wasn't exactly it. Because although Marina didn't have *any* familiar right now, she felt closer to Mom in this moment than in any other time since she'd died . . .

Marina fell asleep to the sound of the ocean waves and her new friends' whispers.

It was a good night.

Tomorrow would be worse.

ROCK THE BOAT

Marina woke with a jolt. The ship was rocking.

And rocking.

And rocking.

And rocking.

It was violent. And the worst part was that Marina could barely see. The sun was just peeking over the horizon. The morning was dusky and dull.

Ember had fallen asleep at the wheel.

"Ember?" Marina cried as she ran to the starboard side. She scanned the water. She was looking for the boat that was following them yesterday. If it was there, Marina couldn't see it. Waves crashed against the SS *Seashanty*. "Ember, help!"

If they didn't do something, the boat might flip over. They would be lost at sea!

The ship lurched. Marina tripped over Hailey and landed on top of Kit.

"AH! DANGER!" Hailey yelped.

"Ugh," Kit groaned. Marina tried to get up, but the boat threw her back on top of Kit. "Marina, this is my least favorite way to wake up. For future reference."

"Sorry!"

Hailey helped Marina to her feet—and away from Kit.

"What's happening?" Hailey asked.

"The waves are really rough. I think the boat might tip—OUCH."

Marina looked down at her palm. It wasn't glowing. It was *burning*. The arrow spun in a circle. Around and around. "My hand!" She held her palm out to Hailey and Kit. "My Mythie must be—"

THUMP.

No. It was more like:
THUMP.

The boat hit something hard. Very hard. Then the butt of the ship began to swivel.

The thud woke Pippa and Ember. "We hit something!" Ember cried.

"Marina's familiar!" Hailey shouted. "Her narwhal!"

Marina nervously twisted her hair. "If it is a narwhal, we thumped its horn! What if I hurt it? What if it hates me now? What if—"

"Marina, for the millionth time, narwhals are *real* animals. Your Mythie won't be a narwhal."

"It could be a narwhale!" Hailey said.

Kit snorted. "A narwhale?"

"You know . . . a whale with a horn."

"That's exactly what a narwhal is!"

"Then a nardolphin," Hailey said matter-of-factly.

"What's a—oh, never mind," Kit said.

Hailey kept talking. She ignored Kit. "Or maybe you have a narstingray, Marina. Or a narotter. Or a narmanatee."

"It doesn't have to be a nar-animal, you know," Ember said.

"Don't bother, Ember. They're too far gone," Kit said. She rolled her eyes.

"Oh no, what if I have a narshark?!" Marina gasped.

"A narshark would be awesome, M!" Hailey said.

"All those teeth!" Marina whimpered, tugging at her hair.

The ship croaked. Its old, creaky bones were stretching.

SNAP.

The SS *Seashanty* broke into two pieces. The middle collapsed. Their boxes of supplies rolled into the sea and sank like stones.

Everyone screamed as they scrambled to a safe

spot. Marina clung to the ship's railing. She closed her eyes tight.

This isn't happening, she thought. *Please don't let this be happening,* she begged.

But it *was* happening.

When Marina opened her eyes again, she was on one side of the ship with Hailey and Pippa. Ember and Kit were on the other side. The ocean separated them.

How could a sturdy ship break? What could have

done it other than a narshark?

"Marina?" Pippa said, panic rising in her voice.

Tentacles curled over the railing. One by one. Then a giant round head popped out of the ocean. The creature's eyes were a glittering black. Its mouth was open and full of sharp teeth. It drooled ocean water.

Marina's heart nearly stopped. The whole world stopped. She couldn't hear anything but a pounding in her ears. She grabbed the railing in horror.

In her brain, she'd known her familiar would be a mythical beast. But she wasn't prepared for just how beastly her beast would be.

And it was a *BEAST*.

Marina's palm radiated light now. She squinted and turned away. Looking at her hand was like staring straight into the sun.

The monster's mouth pulsated. It blinked at her.

"Marina! Wow!" Hailey cried. Her eyes were wide. "You have a naroctopus!"

CREATURE FROM THE DEEP

Why.

Marina had never thought about bonding with an octopus or squid. Why had she never thought about it?

"Let me at it!" Hailey shouted gleefully. She was fired up. "I'll tear it to pieces!"

"Dear, mighty naroctopus!" Pippa said, bowing before it. "We come in peace."

"Ohmygoodness, it's not a naroctopus!" Kit yelled from the other half of the broken ship. "There is no horn on that thing. It's a regular octopus!"

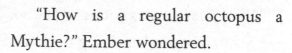

"How is a regular octopus a Mythie?" Ember wondered.

But it wasn't a regular octopus either. Marina knew what it was. Because she was smart. And because she was anxious. And because she was smart enough to be anxious.

She knew exactly what that was. It was called a KRAKEN.

It had tentacles and a bulbous head like an octopus or squid. But the kraken was a hundred times bigger. Their boat would be swallowed in one bite. Each one of its teeth was taller than Marina's whole body. Its ink-black eyes were each the size of Marina's bedroom.

It was blood-chilling. She couldn't believe this was happening.

When Marina was younger, Harbor used to tease her about a kraken emerging from the Seaside Sands ocean to come steal her away.

Her dad assured her that krakens were not real. They were only fiction. Pretend. Make-believe.

Still, Marina used to have nightmares about the kraken. Her nightmares were nothing compared to the monster in front of her. It was so much scarier in real life.

The kraken opened its mouth wide. There were hundreds of glittering teeth inside of a black-hole mouth. It moved closer. Then it bit the mainsail right off the boat.

The metal mast snapped in half like a twig.

With its tentacles, the kraken lifted both sides of the boat clear out of the water.

Kit screamed. "Marina, do something! Marina—wait. Behind us! Not again! We're in major trouble!"

Here, Marina thought, *are all the things that are wrong*:

- The boat was split in two
- With the Mythics separated
- Suspended above the water
- Because her Mythie was a monster
- That she was very afraid of
- And since they followed her palm arrow first, no one else had a familiar that could help her
- And if the kraken didn't drag them down to the bottom of the ocean
- Then each half of their boat was going to sink

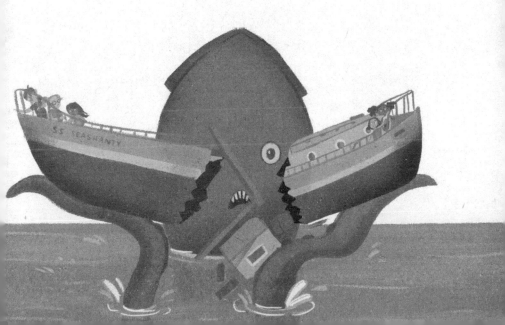

So when Kit said, "We're in major trouble," like they weren't *already* in major trouble, Marina knew it was bad.

She looked behind her.

Major trouble, indeed.

The boat that had been following them yesterday was catching up fast.

It wasn't their families. It was a woman in a gold jumpsuit. She was headed for Marina's Mythie. With a giant cannon aimed right at it.

As if this situation couldn't get any worse!

WHO ARE YOU?

There was no escape for the Mythics. The kraken was too powerful. They were tangled in tentacles. Marina, Ember, Kit, Pippa, and Hailey watched helplessly as Golden Jumpsuit fired her cannon.

BOOM.

A ball flung toward them. It expanded into a net. It missed the kraken. But the monster screeched and dropped both halves of the boat. They plummeted into the water. There was a huge splash. Marina's half of the boat bobbed in place before the kraken wrapped its arms around it again. Across the gap,

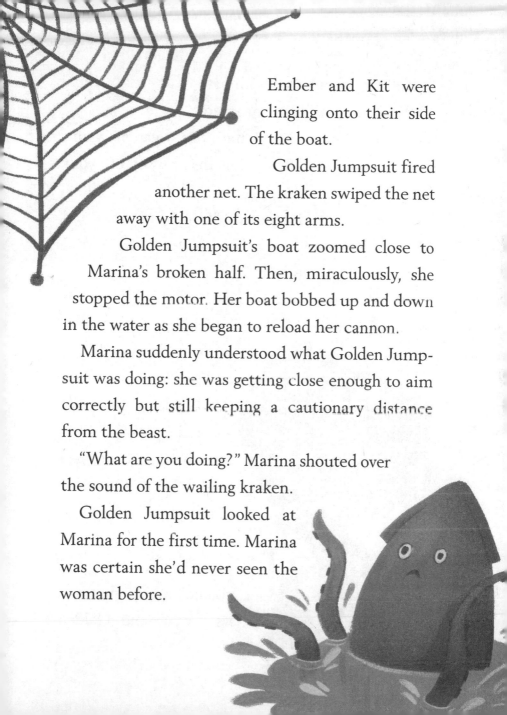

Ember and Kit were clinging onto their side of the boat.

Golden Jumpsuit fired another net. The kraken swiped the net away with one of its eight arms.

Golden Jumpsuit's boat zoomed close to Marina's broken half. Then, miraculously, she stopped the motor. Her boat bobbed up and down in the water as she began to reload her cannon.

Marina suddenly understood what Golden Jumpsuit was doing: she was getting close enough to aim correctly but still keeping a cautionary distance from the beast.

"What are you doing?" Marina shouted over the sound of the wailing kraken.

Golden Jumpsuit looked at Marina for the first time. Marina was certain she'd never seen the woman before.

But her eyes glowed with hatred.

"Who are you?" Marina cried.

Golden Jumpsuit pointed her weapon again. "I'm helping you. By taking that power off your hands."

A cold chill shuddered through Marina, and Mayor Mejor's warning echoed in her head. "Y-you! You're trying to steal my familiar."

"What was your first clue?" Golden Jumpsuit said mockingly.

"Well, stop it . . . please."

Golden Jumpsuit jeered. "Wow, great job, hero. You stopped me." Then she fired another net from the cannon.

The kraken was panicking. It thrashed its arms around. Golden

Jumpsuit held on tight to her boat as it bobbed in a furious wave. Meanwhile, the two halves of the SS *Seashanty* were being spun like teacups on a whirly ride.

"I didn't realize being special came with a side of constant nausea—AHHHHHH!" Kit shrieked as the kraken threw her side of the boat across the ocean. The boat broke apart and flew into the air: an explosion of splinters. Marina did not see Kit or Ember in the rolling waves.

Pippa yelped in horror.

"KIT! EMBER!" Hailey shouted. She turned to Pippa. "We have to save them!"

But there was nothing they could do.

Only *she* could do something. Marina.

But she was frozen in fear.

Golden Jumpsuit took aim with her net cannon.

BOOM!

Another net came out. This time, it tied two of the kraken's arms together. The kraken thrashed. It wiggled its limbs.

"It's panicking," Marina said. "It's scared. Same as me!"

She had a lot more in common with her familiar than she'd realized.

Marina let go of the railing. She climbed over the edge of the ship. And she jumped.

Marina tried to land squarely on the kraken's arm, but it was too slippery. Instead, she slid down like a slide.

She plopped straight into the water.

"Marina!" Pippa cried down to her.

"Oh no," Hailey groaned. "She's walked the plank!"

The water was freezing cold. It got in her mouth and made her lips pucker. Some even got up her nose and made her choke. She knew how to swim—how could she *not*, growing up in Seaside Sands?—but she was never able to lose herself in the waves. Especially not when the water was deep.

And now the bottom of the sea was thousands of feet below her. Who knew what lurked in the darkness of the ocean? She didn't want creatures moving beneath her, but emptiness stretching for miles below was just as alarming.

But Marina couldn't—*wouldn't*—think about it. She had to reach the kraken, so she kept moving forward. She swam and swam and swam. The ocean waves were rough. She kicked and paddled.

She had only one thought in her brain: get to the kraken.

There was no time for fear or worry. Her Mythie needed her.

Her panicked paddles turned into smooth glides. For a moment, she forgot about all the scary parts of the ocean. She stopped fighting the waves and moved with them, like she'd seen her parents do, like Harbor did. For once, the water wasn't something to struggle against—the water was something to guide her. This was swimming like she had never swum before. And she took to it like, well, a fish to water.

Golden Jumpsuit released another net that tied three more of the kraken's arms together. The kraken wailed.

"I've almost got you now, you terrible beast!" Golden Jumpsuit said.

The kraken twisted and twitched.

"Stop!" Marina screamed. She was out of breath. Her lungs were on fire, and her legs were sore. But still, she swam like mad. "It doesn't want to go with you!"

Golden Jumpsuit sneered. "I don't care what it wants. I'm doing what's best for—"

"GET AWAY!" Marina yelled. Salty water got in her mouth, but she didn't care. She had to help her Mythie. She had to do *something*.

BOOM.

Golden Jumpsuit's net came out again. It narrowly missed.

The kraken wailed. Marina had no idea that something that looked so terrifying could be so terrified itself. But there were no rules to fear.

Except this: only love could dissolve it. Marina had to prove that the kraken could trust her. Only then could they work together against their common enemy.

Golden Jumpsuit loaded another net, and Marina swam, swam, swam.

She reached the kraken at last. Marina looked up into its frightened eyes. She felt connected. The kraken belonged to her, and she belonged to the kraken. They belonged to each other. It was like having an instant best friend.

"It's going to be okay," Marina said, putting her glowing palm on its limb. The Mythic and her familiar both began to glow.

And then they morphed.

THE BOND

There was a loud buzzing in Marina's head. She felt like she was stretching as far as she could. She was putty being pulled. She was pizza dough being kneaded.

"What is happening?" Marina cried. Only her voice didn't work. It sounded very much like a series of bubbly blubs.

She reached out her arms—she had eight of them. She looked around. Golden Jumpsuit was hundreds of feet below her eye level.

"I'm inside the kraken!" Marina blubbed. "No, I

am the kraken!" This never happened to her dad and
Crabby. Or Harbor and Sea Lion. What was *happening*
to her? She didn't know whether to rejoice or panic.

Panic sounded good. *HELP!* she tried to cry.
"BLUB!" she blubbed.

"Marina!" Pippa called. "Marina! Hailey, where
did she go?"

"She disappeared!"

I'm right here! Marina tried to shout. "Blub-blub-blub!"

In the back of her mind, she felt a comforting life force beside her. She knew it was the kraken. Marina thought of it, and it thought of her. And it was like their spirits were hugging. They were a team now.

Marina and her Mythie. Marina and the other Mythics.

Golden Jumpsuit looked nervous. She paused to stare. Then she put a hand on her cannon.

Marina had to stop Golden Jumpsuit. Her arms were still tied. So she swirled in the water. Around and around in a circle, until the water formed a whirlpool.

The whirlpool was sucking in Golden Jumpsuit's boat. Marina spat out a stream of salt water. It was like a hose. It hit Golden Jumpsuit and knocked her off her dinghy.

"I'll get you!" Golden Jumpsuit shouted as she flailed in the water. "I'm more powerful than you think, Mythic. You may win the day, but I will win eternity!"

Good luck, Marina thought, braver than she felt.

Then Marina used her three free arms to unwrap her five netted ones.

Then she raised all eight of her limbs to create a

giant wave. It was bigger than big. It was a tsunami. Golden Jumpsuit was still thrashing as she was swept up in the wave.

And then Marina pushed. And the wave took Golden Jumpsuit far, far away. When the water calmed, Golden Jumpsuit was all alone in the middle of the ocean. She screamed furiously into the sky—and kicked a tantrum on the water.

But Marina didn't care to worry about Golden Jumpsuit anymore. With one arm, Marina grabbed Hailey. With the second, she held Pippa. Marina glided over to the spot where the kraken had thrown the other half of the ship.

Ember was floating on her back. Marina scooped her up. Kit was desperately holding on to a wooden plank that had splintered off from the mayor's boat. Marina plucked her out of the water.

Four arms for four Mythics. With the other four arms, she swam with all her might. She summoned giant waves to push them all the way across the ocean.

And onto shore.

Ember, Pippa, Kit, and Hailey were panting on the gravelly, rocky beach. Kit coughed up water. Ember pulled three fish out of her pant leg. Marina was still, somehow, the kraken. She panted hard, her suckers sticking tight to a giant rock.

"Where's Marina?" Ember asked.

"Marina!" Kit cried, running ankle-deep into the water. "Did we lose her at sea? The mayor's boat—it sunk. You don't think Marina was on it, do you?"

"No," Pippa said. "We watched her jump off the boat and swim toward her Mythie."

Hailey wailed. "Oh no! I bet she was eaten by the kraken! Cough her up, you beast! I'll fight you!

I'll bite you! Duel me, you monster! Don't worry, Marina! We'll cut open its stomach—"

Marina recoiled. They weren't going to touch her—or her Mythie!

As Hailey, Ember, and Kit debated what to do next, Pippa adjusted her glasses and looked up at Marina. They locked eyes. There was something about Pippa's stare—first curious, then concerned—that made Marina know Pippa truly saw *her*, and not just the monster she'd become.

"Everyone, look at the kraken's eyes," Pippa said, her voice as gentle as always. "I think . . . this *is* Marina. Are you in there, Marina?"

Yes—it's me! Marina tried to say. "Blub-blub-blub!" A stream of water escaped her mouth.

The other Mythics looked at each other, worried.

Am I doomed to be a sea kraken forever?

Marina thought. *Is this what being a Mythic is? Would she live her life on the ocean floor with all sorts of nar-creatures?*

Marina was full-on panicking. *I never asked for this! And now I'm a monster! How do I get out of here? I want to get out of here!*

Marina felt like she was burning up with fever. The spirit of the kraken began to stir beside her. She wasn't unbonded, but she felt ill and clammy. The more she tried to wriggle out of the bond, the more their spirits fused tight . . . and the more nauseated she felt. Her panic—her fear—was only making their situation worse.

Then Marina remembered: it was love and trust that bonded them together. Could that be the secret power that would restore their individual selves too?

She took a deep breath. Her heart stopped racing. When she calmed down, Marina could feel the warmth of her bond with the kraken.

Then, instantly, they unfused. She was herself again.

Two arms, two legs, no suckers.

Ember gasped.

"What was that?! What did you—how did you—" Hailey shouted. "Marina, you are a giant kraken!"

"*Was* a giant kraken," corrected Kit. "But still . . . wow!"

"How do you feel?" Pippa asked.

Marina looked around for her kraken. It was gone. She felt a sudden and unexpected heartache. "Where is it?" she cried.

"Look! There!" Ember said.

Hiding behind a rock was the kraken. But mini! It wiggled over to Marina and crawled up her back. It stopped when it got to her head. Marina looked like she was wearing a tiny octopus as a hat.

"What is *happening*?" Marina yelped. "Get it off me, get it off me!"

Kit and Pippa tried to pull it off, but the kraken

held on tight. It suckled her head. Marina felt like a juice box.

"On the plus side," Kit said, "maybe kraken spit is a nice shampoo."

"Why isn't the kraken enormous anymore?" Ember asked.

Marina had an answer for this. "I think . . . it's a baby. But it can expand when it needs to. Fear can make it grow."

She was beginning to understand why the kraken resembled her, and she it. Fear sometimes swelled inside of them, and anxiety made them squirm. But even more than that: Marina knew the kraken was a cephalopod, like an octopus or a squid. Now that she was thinking about it, she couldn't imagine a better familiar for herself. Cephalopods—and Marina—were smart, eager for connection, and able to problem-solve.

And speaking of problem-solving, Marina knew they had to put as much distance between them and Golden Jumpsuit as possible. "We should head away from the ocean." Marina pointed to the trees ahead of them. A jet of water accidentally came out of her finger and squirted Kit in the face. "Ooops! Sorry."

"I've had enough of water, thank you!" Kit said as she wrung out her hair.

"Wait, Marina, what was that?" Ember asked. "Can you do it again?"

Marina wiggled her fingers, and water began to form into a sphere in her hand, but then the sphere collapsed into a puddle between her fingers.

"Water powers," Kit said. Her eyes twinkled with desire. "I am jealous!"

"Our Mythie bonds come with powers?" Ember said.

"But it seems like we'll have to practice to get control of them. I can barely water a plant right now."

"You watered my face just fine," Kit grumbled.

"I believe in you, Marina," Pippa said encouragingly. "You'll figure it out."

"Water powers are awesome," Hailey said. "But nothing compares to when Marina *literally became a kraken of the sea*! When I get my awesome Mythie of awesomeness, I need you to teach me that."

"I don't know what I did," Marina admitted. "I just did it."

"Well, you are my SHERO!" Hailey said. She held Marina's right hand and turned her palm over.

Marina's glowing arrow was gone. Instead, there was a glowing star.

"Wow!" they all marveled.

Without saying anything, the other four Mythics turned their own palms over. Different directions, all of them.

"Who's next?" Marina asked.

"Me!" they all said.

Everyone laughed.

"Remember when you didn't want to be special, Marina?" Kit said. "So . . . how do you feel now?"

"Honestly? I'm glad my quest is over. I have never been so terrified."

"But you were brilliant," Ember said. "Maybe you were terrified, but you overcame it."

The compliment was nice. But Marina knew it wasn't correct. And they had promised to be honest with each other. "I wish that were true, Ember, but I didn't. I never got over my fear," Marina said. "I just . . . got through it. I think I'll always be anxious. I don't know how not to be."

"That's okay," Pippa said, squeezing Marina's shoulders. "Everything you are and everything you feel is okay. We like you just the way you are."

"Yeah. You wouldn't be you if you weren't a worrywart!" Kit teased. She stuck her tongue out.

"Don't ever change!" Hailey said. "Except when you can be a literal kraken of the sea. Then you definitely should change."

The kraken wiggled its arms, and Marina smiled. She stared out into the sea. She hoped her dad and Harbor would be proud of her. She had her Mythie, but she still might not see them for a while.

It was her duty to help her friends. To protect them from danger.

And danger promised it would come again.

"I'm afraid Golden Jumpsuit will come after us," Marina said.

"See? She's right back to worrying!" Kit teased.

Ember frowned. "Who was that woman?"

"She said she wanted to help . . . by taking the power off my hands."

"Then she didn't want to help," Ember said darkly. "And I think we'll see her again. Don't you?"

They all nodded.

"If it's power she wants, then she'll follow us," Marina said. She had thought about this a lot and had come up with the answer. "We have the arrows, pointing the way. If she wants our Mythies, she'll get to them through us."

"But who is she?" Hailey asked. "Where did she come from? Who told her about the Mythics and the Mythies? How did she know to find us in the ocean? What is her endgame? Why does she wear a golden jumpsuit? And where can I get one?"

These were all good questions. No one had answers.

"It doesn't matter," Ember said. "It doesn't change what we have to do. We have to keep going. We have four more mythical beasts to find!"

"I wonder what ours could be," Pippa said dreamily.

"Only one way to find out," Hailey said, bouncing with excitement. "Let's go!"

Marina, Hailey, Kit, Ember, and Pippa walked toward a thicket of trees. Laughing. Palms glowing. Ready for whatever came next.

TO BE CONTINUED

ACKNOWLEDGMENTS

EDITOR
Ben Rosenthal

EDITORIAL
Julia Johnson
Tanu Srivastava

DESIGN
Laura Mock
Amy Ryan

WRITERS HOUSE
Alexandra Levick
Cecilia de la Campa
Alessandra Birch
Jessica Berger
Jenissa Graham

Sofia Bolido
Brianne Johnson

BRIGHT AGENCY
James Burns
Alex Gehringer

PUBLISHER
Katherine Tegen

PUBLICITY
Mitch Thorpe

MANAGING EDITORIAL
Mark Rifkin
Kathryn Silsand

PRODUCTION
Nicole Moulaison
Annabelle Sinoff

PROOFREADING
Janet Rosenberg
Kristen Eberhard
Susan Bishansky

DIGITAL MARKETING
Mariner Brito
Sam Fox
Maureen Germain
Colleen O'Connell
Chris Pena
Farah Reza
Sonia Sells
Emily Zhu

MARKETING
Ann Dye
Robby Imfeld
Nellie Kurtzman
Emily Mannon
Anais Villa Gray
Lexie Axon

SCHOOL & LIBRARY MARKETING
Katie Dutton
Mimi Rankin
Patty Rosati
Christina Carpino
Josie Dallam

SALES
Jessica Abel
Doris Allen
Heather Doss
Megan Carr
Kathy Faber
Emily Logan
Kerry Moynagh
Andrea Pappenheimer
Jennifer Wygand
Susan Yeager

AUDIO
Almeda Beynon
Caitlin Garing